Some Things You Should
Know About Goblins

Gaggles
Seven Goblins make a Gaggle.
Not six. Not eight. Seven.

Hats
Goblins always wear woolly
hats with bobbles. They are
very proud of them.

Favourite Food
Sausages.

Favourite Sweets
Gobblegum.
And gobstoppers.

Goblin Babies
They eat *anything*.

Kaye Umansky

GOBLiNZ!
DETECTIVES INC.

illustrated by Andi Good

PUFFIN BOOKS

PUFFIN BOOKS

Published by the Penguin Group
Penguin Books Ltd, 80 Strand, London WC2R 0RL, England
Penguin Group (USA), Inc., 375 Hudson Street, New York, New York 10014, USA
Penguin Books Australia Ltd, 250 Camberwell Road, Camberwell, Victoria 3124, Australia
Penguin Books Canada Ltd, 10 Alcorn Avenue, Toronto, Ontario, Canada M4V 3B2
Penguin Books India (P) Ltd, 11 Community Centre, Panchsheel Park, New Delhi – 110 017, India
Penguin Books (NZ) Ltd, Cnr Rosedale and Airborne Roads, Albany, Auckland, New Zealand
Penguin Books (South Africa) (Pty) Ltd, 24 Sturdee Avenue, Rosebank 2196, South Africa

Penguin Books Ltd, Registered Offices: 80 Strand, London WC2R 0RL, England

www.penguin.com

First published in Puffin Books 2004
1 3 5 7 9 10 8 6 4 2

Text copyright © Kaye Umansky, 2004
Illustrations copyright © Andi Good, 2004
All rights reserved

The moral right of the author and illustrator has been asserted

Set in Monotype Times New Roman Schoolbook 22 on 14.5pt

Printed in China by Midas Printing Ltd

British Library Cataloguing in Publication Data
A CIP catalogue record for this book is available from the British Library

ISBN 0–141–31501–6

Contents

1. What Shy Saw

Shy the Goblin came hurrying down the lane. There was a Gaggle meeting and he was late. His mum had made him come back and button his coat properly.

It was a windy day and she didn't
want him catching cold.

Shy's Gaggle was called the
Goblineers. They had a Club House
and a Secret Sign and everything.
They were Shy's best friends.

The lane led past Two Trees
Cottage, where Arthur Greenmangle
the Dwarf lived. Arthur took great
pride in his garden. The front was full
of flowers. In the back, he grew
vegetables. Every year, Arthur won
the cup for Best Marrow. It stood

proudly on his mantelpiece. Right
now, he was away, judging a
gardening show in another village.

Arthur didn't like the Goblineers,
ever since they had tried to do a good
deed by trimming his cherry trees.

Shy glanced guiltily at the two bald stumps on either side of the gate. They still hadn't grown. There was a new sign on the gate. It said:

NO GOOD DEEDS THANKS

Just then, a gust of wind snatched off his hat and blew it away, over the neat hedge. Oh dear. He would be later than ever, but he had to get his hat back.

Shy pushed open the gate and stepped into the perfect garden.

The hat had landed in the flower bed
over by the window.

Carefully, he tiptoed across the
beautifully mown lawn. He was just
bending down for his hat when he
heard something.

A floorboard creaked inside the cottage. Then there was a cough. Oh, no! Arthur wasn't away after all!

Slowly, Shy stood up and peered through the window. He couldn't see very well, because the window sill was full of pot plants. Inside, a short, shadowy shape moved about, holding something large and shiny.

Shy ducked back down and dived for the shelter of a nearby bush.

Moments later, the front door opened – and out stepped a short figure with a sack on his back. He was a Dwarf, all right, but he wasn't Arthur. Arthur had a big beard, not rough stubble. Arthur wore a pointy hat, not a flat cap.

Shy squeezed further into the bush. His heart was thumping.

The strange Dwarf turned up his collar, pulled his cap down, then scuttled along the path and out the gate.

Shy waited until the footsteps had died away – then ran for it.

2. In the Club House

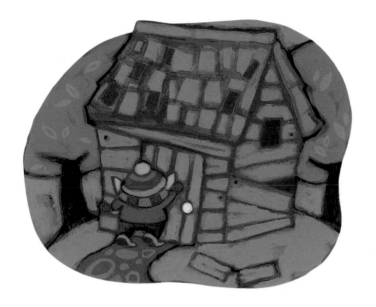

The Club House was an old shed in the woods. Shy came panting up and banged on the door.

"Password," commanded a voice.

"Sausages!" gasped Shy.

The door opened and Oggy looked out.
"Enter, Goblineer," he said.
Shy fell inside and collapsed on to
the nearest upturned bucket.

They were all there – Oggy, Tuf,
Cloreen Gobbles, Wheels, Twinge and
his little brother, Grizzle.

Cloreen had brought sweets, as usual. Everyone's cheeks bulged with gobstoppers, except for Grizzle's. His were bulging with coal.

"Hello, Shy," said Tuf. "You look all puffed out."

"I am," panted Shy. "Listen, I've just seen …"

"Shouldn't we do the Secret Sign first?" said Twinge. "Now we're all here?"

"Oh. Yes, of course," said Shy shyly. After all, the Secret Sign had been his idea.

Everyone stood up.

"The Goblineers," they said solemnly, pulling on their ears. Grizzle pulled his nose, because he was little.

"So what did you see?" asked
Cloreen. She gave Shy a gobstopper.

"Well, you see, I was walking past
Two Trees Cottage …"

And he explained all about it.
When he had finished, there was a
pause.

"So it wasn't Mr Greenmangle,
den?" said Tuf slowly. He liked to
get his facts straight.

"No. A strange Dwarf, like I said."

"And he was carrying something shiny, you say?" asked Oggy.

"Yes. I couldn't see well. But you know what? I think it was Arthur's Best Marrow cup. The big silver one on his mantelpiece. I think he was a robber.

Arthur never locks his door. The strange Dwarf just walked in and helped himself to the cup. I expect he'll melt it down for the silver."

"Oooh! How wicked!" said Cloreen, clutching hold of Oggy, who shoved her away.

"You know what?" said Shy. "This is a job for the Goblineers. It's our chance to make it up."

"I is not allowed to make fings up," said Tuf sadly.

"No, I mean make it up to Arthur. For cutting his trees down."

The Goblineers still felt very sorry about Arthur's cherry trees.

"How?" asked Twinge.

"We'll get his cup back," said Shy simply. "We'll be detectives. Look for clues. The robber might have dropped something. A bit of paper with his address on."

"Why? Doesn't he know where he lives?" asked Tuf, amazed. Even *he* knew that.

"Footprints, then. Anything that helps us find the cup. Just think how pleased Arthur will be."

"He might even say sorry for shouting at us like that," agreed Wheels. "My ears are still ringing. Vrrrrmmmm!"

"What do we need to be detectives?"
Oggy wanted to know.

"A notebook," said Shy. "And a torch. And a magnifying glass. Sometimes they wear disguises, like big hats. Even their own mothers don't know them."

Everyone imagined walking by their own mothers without being recognized. It sounded fun.

"What's a monkey – manky – dat fing you said?" asked Tuf.

"A magnifying glass. It makes the clues bigger. I've got one at home."

"I've got a torch," said Wheels. "It doesn't work, though. Vrrrrrm."

"I've got a big hat," said Cloreen. "I'll go and get it, shall I?"

"Good idea," agreed Oggy. "And more sweets while you're about it."

"We should all go," decided Shy. "We'll go home and get useful detective stuff. Then we'll meet outside Arthur's cottage. But don't tell anyone. This is our case. We don't want anyone spoiling things."

3. Detecting

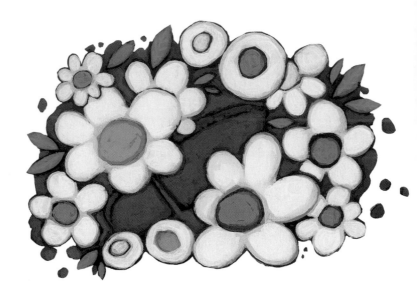

"See anything?" whispered Twinge.

"No," said Shy. "It's too dark."

They stood in a group, peering through Arthur Greenmangle's

window. Oggy had an old notebook.
Wheels had his broken torch. Shy had
a magnifying glass. Cloreen wore a
big, floppy hat with a flower on.
Twinge wore a curly wig belonging to
his mum. Tuf had a plastic
moustache. Grizzle was eating grass.

"I've found a clue," hissed Wheels,
pointing his torch at the flower bed.
"Look! A footprint!"

"That's mine, actually," said Shy.

"Dare we go in and have a look?" asked Cloreen.

"I think we'll have to," decided Shy. "Make sure you wipe your feet."

Moments later, they stood in the front room, staring at the empty space on the mantelpiece.

"You see?" said Shy. "It's gone."

"He really likes plants, doesn't he?" said Cloreen, looking around. "I don't know how he moves in here."

"Look what I've found!" called Twinge. "There's a cardboard box in the hall. It's full of Arthur's clothes and stuff."

"Hey!" gasped Oggy, pointing at a large, green vegetable which was propped next to the door.

"That must be this year's prize marrow! Wow! It's huge!"

Suddenly, to their horror, there came the sound of approaching footsteps!

"Hide!" gasped Shy.

Everybody dived behind the sofa, just in time.

The front door creaked open. Someone entered the hall.

There was a short pause, then the door closed again and the footsteps hurried away down the path.

Seven heads poked up from behind the sofa.

"Now he's stolen the box," said Shy grimly. "Come on."

"Why? What we gonna do?" asked Tuf.

"Trail him, of course."

"Will it take long?" Tuf fingered his moustache, which clipped on to his nose in a painful way.

"Depends where his hideout is. Quick, before we lose him."

4. Trailing

The robber Dwarf scurried down the lane, the box in his arms. The Goblineers followed at a safe distance, keeping close to the hedge. After a few minutes, the

Dwarf climbed over a stile and took off into the woods.

It was easier to trail him there, with all those trees to hide behind. Trying not to breathe, the Goblineers crept along. Twinge fed Grizzle twigs to keep him quiet.

Before long, the trees thinned out. In a clearing stood a small house. In the garden was a tiny shed.

Just then, a voice called
from inside the house.
"Is that you, Ted?"
"Yes," shouted the Dwarf.

He set down the box by the shed and took a key from his pocket.

"Did you get the stuff?"

"Yes. I'm sticking it in the shed."

"Well, hurry up. The fire's going nicely."

The Dwarf got the door open and placed the box inside. He locked the shed again and went into the house.

"Did you hear that?" whispered Shy, peering out from behind a tree.

"They've got a fire to melt down the cup!"

"Where *is* the cup, I wonder?" said Oggy.

"Hidden in the shed," said Shy promptly. "I saw the sack when he opened the door. Come on."

Silently, they crept into the garden.

The shed, though small, was solid. The Goblineers tried pushing at the door, but it was hopeless.

"There's an open window,"
whispered Oggy, coming from round
the back. "But none of us is small
enough to squeeze in."

"Grizzle is," said Twinge. Everyone
looked down at Grizzle, who was
sitting on the grass, eating daisies.

"Will he do it, though?" said
Wheels doubtfully.

"We could try." Twinge knelt down
next to his brother. "Hey, Grizzle!"

Grizzle looked up, his mouth full of
chewed petals.

"Ga?"

"Listen. We're going to put you in
the window. You've got to go and
get the big sack and bring it to us,
right?"

"Ga," said Grizzle, then screamed as Twinge yanked him away from the daisies. "Gagagagagagagagagagaga ..."

"All right, all right, take them with you." Twinge tore up a clump of daisies and stuffed them in Grizzle's dirty hand. Everyone moved round to the back of the shed, out of sight of the house.

Twinge hoisted Grizzle up to the

window and stuffed him in, feet first.

There came a thump.

"Good boy," hissed Twinge, peering through. "Now. Get the sack."

There was a longish pause.

"What's happening?" whispered Shy.

"He's doing it, I think. No, he isn't. He's seen a pile of turnips. No, Grizzle! Not turnips! The sack!"

"Is he getting it now?"

"No. Grizzle! Will you get that sack? Oh, bother. He's found a bag of birdseed that he loves."

"Will he be long, do you fink?" asked Tuf. "Because dis moustache disguise is hurting my nose a *lot*."

"Grizzle!" hissed Twinge. "If you get the sack, Cloreen will give you a gobstopper. Even though you're not allowed."

"Ga?" came a small voice from inside.

"Yes, I promise. Just get the sack!"

"Is he doing it now?" fretted Shy, hopping from foot to foot.

"I think so. Good, Grizzle. Come to Twinge. Pass it up. Yes, I know it's heavy."

From the house, there came the sound of a banging door.

"I'm going back for the marrow!" came the Dwarf's voice.

"Oh, are you indeed?" muttered Shy. "Not if I can help it. Grizzle, come *on!*"

A moment later, the top of the sack appeared through the window. Twinge reached in and hauled it out, with Grizzle clinging to the bottom.

"Right," gasped Shy. "Let's go!"

5. Protecting the Marrow

"So what's the plan?" gasped Oggy, as they burst from the trees and raced up the lane.

"We've got to protect the marrow," panted Shy. "Wheels, you're the fastest.

Go and get the policeman! The rest of us will lock ourselves into Arthur's cottage."

"Vrrrrrmmmm!" agreed Wheels, and whizzed off at top speed.

Minutes later, the remaining six were running to and fro, busily stacking furniture behind Arthur's front door. They used chairs, small tables and Arthur's hatstand. Tuf pushed the big grandfather clock across the hall. It left nasty scratches on the floor.

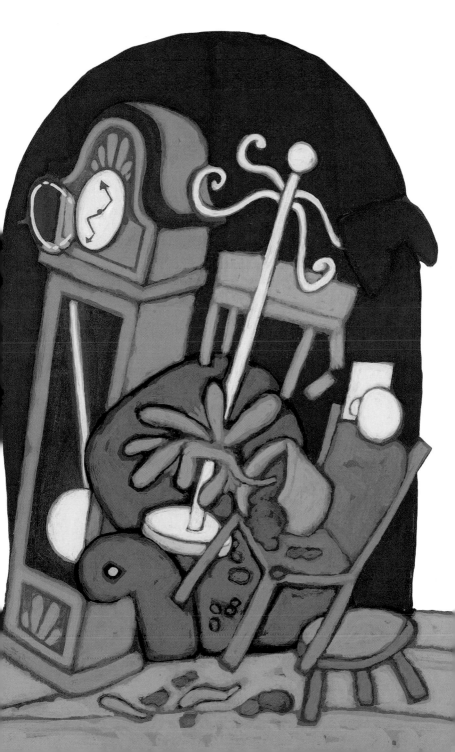

They put the marrow and the sack
with the cup in it in the front room
for safety. They put Grizzle there as
well because he was getting under
everyone's feet.

"Let's use the sofa," said Cloreen.
"He'll never shift that, will he?"

Tuf took one end of the sofa and
Oggy and Shy took the other.
Twinge went to stop Grizzle from

emptying Arthur's plant pots on to
the carpet.

"One, two, three!" shouted Oggy.
They lifted the sofa and tottered
across the room, knocking over more
plants in the process. They got it
partly through the doorway, then it
stuck.

They were just getting their breath
back and wondering what to do,

when there came the sound of voices
from outside.

The Goblineers went pale.

Footsteps stopped outside the front
door. There was a short pause. Then
a familiar voice said, "That's funny.
It seems to be stuck."

"Arthur!" shouted Shy. "He's
back!"

Eagerly, he ran to the window,
undid the catch and threw it open.
A flowering geranium crashed to
the floor.

"Over here, Mr Greenmangle! It's us! A wicked robber came and he took your cup and lots of your stuff and he's coming back for your ma ..."

His voice died away.

Out in the garden stood Arthur Greenmangle. In his arms was the Best Marrow cup. With him was the robber Dwarf!

"You again!" said Arthur. He sounded furious.

"I don't get it," said the robber Dwarf. "Who are they?"

"Those Goblins I told you about. The ones who ruined my cherry trees. And now they've gone and wrecked my house! Just look at the state of it! Where's all the furniture? What do you think you're doing with my sofa? *And why is that baby eating my plants?*"

"Ga," said Grizzle, through a mouthful of geranium.

"I don't understand," wailed Shy. "What are you doing with the robber?"

"Robber, my foot! This is my cousin Ted. He came round to water my plants while I was away."

"That's right," agreed Ted.

"And to pick up the box of stuff Arthur left out for the jumble sale."

"But we thought – well, the cup was missing, and we thought –"

"Missing?" spluttered Arthur. "Of course it was missing! I took it with me, to have my name put on it."

"Den what's in de sack?" asked Tuf, puzzled.

Cloreen marched over to the corner

Arthur Greenmangle
BEST MARROW

where they had left the sack and
pulled it open.

"Uh-oh," she said. And took out –
a large, shiny watering can!

"It's mine," said Ted. "Arthur's has
sprung a leak."

"But the marrow!" protested Shy.
"He said he was taking your prize
marrow!"

"Why not?" said Ted. "Arthur
doesn't like the taste, do you, Arthur?
Me and the missus love stuffed
marrow."

Just then, to make things even

worse, there came the sound of
skates. The gate burst open and
Wheels came zooming up the path,
with a stout policeman puffing along
behind him!

"Just the person I want to see,"
said Arthur Greenmangle grimly.

6. How It Ended

T he Goblineers sat in the Club
House, mournfully inspecting
their sore hands.

"I really hate cleaning," sighed
Oggy. "I never thought we'd get the

earth off that carpet."

"What about carrying all that furniture, then?" said Cloreen, rubbing her aching back.

"It'll take weeks of pocket money to pay for all those plants Grizzle ate," sighed Wheels. "Vrrrmmm!"

Everyone looked accusingly at Grizzle, who was back on the coal again.

"He's potty for plants," said Twinge.

"He's plant pot-ty," said Cloreen.

Everyone giggled.

"Can we stop being detectives now?" begged Oggy.

"Yes," sighed Shy. "I think we can."

Tuf removed the moustache from his upper lip and gave a sigh of relief.

"Dat's better," he said. "Who wants to come back to my house for sausages?"

Everybody did.